I0782176

CONTENTS

PROLOGUE

Richard and Barbara Hill moved from Massachusetts to Nevada in the early sixties. They built a home there and started a family. It was on a large piece of land with plenty of room to expand. They started raising chickens and selling eggs. The climate was quite a bit different from back east. It was not nearly as humid. Richard's parents had tapped Maple trees and shipped Maple syrup and candy through a mail order business. It was only natural for their son to bring Sugar Maples with him to Nevada. He also took some cuts off an original, Concord Grape vine from the city for which they were named. He put in an irrigation system to the Maples and grapes. After a couple of decades, the home was passed on to Robert Hill and his wife, Mary. Mary gave birth to identical twins shortly after they moved into the house. They called them Melody and Symphony, why? Because shortly after the second one was born, whenever one would cry, so would the other and their crying would almost always harmonize, one baby voice blending with the other. It also came in rhythm's, first one and then the other before blending it all together. Somewhere in the archives there is a crying duet illustrating this very unique sound.

The girls were indeed musical. That was evident from a very early age. Their parents did all they could to encourage this. In time the girls formed a band composed of themselves and five other local girls. They did well so far as small, local bands go. They played for school events, even picked up a wedding or two and a baby shower now and then. Every now and again they put together a gig down town which netted them a few dollars and their names in the paper. It wasn't really about the money, though but more about having fun. Life was good back then. The twins were inseparable up until their teens. They did everything together and nothing apart. Melody was the boldest of the two, always trying to push the boundaries while Symphony held back and tried to keep her sister from going over the edge. It worked some of the time.

On their thirteenth birthday they had their first taste of alcohol. Danny brought some to their party and the three went out behind the chicken coop to try it. Danny's dad owned a liquor store and was an alcoholic, so it was not hard for his son to get his hands on some. Neither Melody nor Symphony liked the taste of it, the younger twin decided to never drink again but not Melody. She chose to develop a taste for it no matter what. To do this she continued to hang out with Danny over the next few years, drinking whenever she got the chance. Alcohol was not enough for Danny. He introduced his girlfriend to drugs. This worried Symphony. She had many talks with her sister about it. A little before the accident that took Melody's life, it seemed like Symphony was getting through to her and making some progress. She got a promise that she would not drink any alcoholic beverages on the very night she was killed in the car crash and according to Danny, she kept her promise. As for the grapes? Only one plant survived of the dozen Concord plants Grandpa brought from back east.

The grape is an interesting fruit. You can enjoy it fresh from the vine or you can take the juice and ferment it. Alcohol is a killer. It is tempting to drink at social events and even have a cold one or more with friends. It is also the popular thing to do among kids as well as adults. It seems harmless enough but if you allow it to get a hold of you, it will eventually take you down. Life is a very precious gift. Unfortunately, many never come to realize that until it is too late. In this short story the reader or listener needs to know there are graphic word descriptions of disturbing things that happened. Know however in reality, the actual alcohol related death is far worse than anyone can describe in a book. To see it for real right in front of you will leave a picture in your mind that can never be erased, especially if it is your twin sister. When you look down at that closed casket and the realization that you will never see her again finally hits home, what then? Can there be any happy endings from such a tragic start to this little book, "The Song of the Grape?"

CHAPTER 1
The Vertical Empire

Symphony sat in Biology class trying to concentrate on what the teacher was explaining. It was especially difficult today. Her mind kept going back to the tragedy that had changed the life of her and her parents forever. It had been six months since that wintery night, but it seemed like only yesterday. Try as she did the trauma of the event would not give her any relief. She was plagued by it in her waking hours as well as in her dreams. Melody would come calling out to her. The sister would run toward her to grab her, but she was always just out of reach. In these dreams her subconscious mind tried to convince her that if she could even once grab that bloody, outstretched hand, her sister would be restored to her. They would again run through the flower carpeted meadow just beyond the giant maple trees or hit the mounds on the dusty dirt bike trails. In the fall they would rough and tumble in the piles of fallen leaves. They would again take up their guitars, Melody on the bass and Symphony on the old electric and sing late into the night. They would make such beautiful music together. But alas she was gone, so the lonely twin was only half alive. Part of her had been severed, cut away forever and the pain was excruciating.

"Photosynthesis is the process by which green plants and some other organisms use sunlight to synthesize foods from carbon dioxide and water. Photosynthesis in plants generally involves the green pigment chlorophyll and generates oxygen as a byproduct." The voice of the professor Brown droned on and on. Several other students were alike somewhere else during this lecture, anywhere but there in Biology. Finally, the class bell rang signaling the day was over. All the other kids would go home to a normal life, all except Symphony. She would be returning once again to an empty room. On this particular day however, she decided to stretch herself out in the hammock under the old arbor. An ancient grape vine had taken up residence there. Her roots went deep into mother earth and her uppermost vines stretched nearly twenty feet in the air. The leaves were fully formed but the old lady bore little fruit. Symphony could see two tiny grapes way up top where one branch managed to reach out to the sun. in a few weeks they would be ripe. The young lady wondered what kind they were. Try as she might she could never remember eating any fruit from here before.

As she lay there rocking in her own sorrow it seemed as if the vine reached her arms down and enfolded the girl. It was comforting. A cardinal and his mate had made a nest in the old Arborvitae. He was perched there keeping watch for some little ones were about ready to try their wings. He warbled the sweetest music Symphony had ever heard. What a soloist he made. If only he could take the lead voice in their band, the whole world might stop by to listen. But he was only a bird. There was a brilliant red flash as he spotted a worm peaking up from the ground after the little shower had sent some droplets of water down his hole. Some babies were about to be very happy. With the buzzing of the bees and the gentle breeze rocking her, the weary twin was lulled to sleep. It was about time to. Perhaps there would be no bad dreams of her sister to trouble her this afternoon.

Symphony found herself in an entirely new world. She had entered an empire filled with music. The very air rang with it. The inhabitants of this strange place went around singing. Deep from down in the ground there was a steady beat that gave a romantic rhythm to the melody that was now playing. This empire did not spread out across miles and mile of land as one would expect but towered into the heavens. There were tubes she could enter and be propelled at near lightning speed to the top or somewhere in the middle even the bottom. Everywhere she went the music was there. She allowed herself to merge with it. It entered in and filled the empty place in her soul. Melody was everywhere in this place of wonder. After checking it all out she stopped to talk with some of the residents of this place. They did not look like humans although they had all the features of a person. They had a head, eyes, nose, mouth, and ears. They used all five senses even as she did. And they could speak her language or perhaps in this empire she could speak theirs. A short female dressed in a lacy blue robe came over to speak with her. She almost sang as she talked. Her voice was light and tinkled almost like a bell. Symphony bent down toward her to listen closely.

"Have you gone to visit the Queen, Symphony," the tinkling bell asked as she raised and lowered her pitch to keep up with the song that was playing?

"How do you know my name; may I call you bell?"

"You can if you like," tinkled the little one. "I have never been a bell. I like that name though, and what were you thinking? Did I hear tinkle? I really do not have a name. Can I be called 'Tinkle Bell? I would like that very much."

"Do any of your kind have names," the young lady asked as she looked around at some of the other beings that were moving around her?

"No, none of us were named. Would you like to name us? I think we would like to have a name. Usually, we just do our own thing. The music tells us what to do and gives us our role to play. What would you name him?" Symphony looked at the little one again before she asked another question. Could she really name anyone without knowing at least something about them?

"If you called that one him does that mean you have hims and hers?"

"Oh, yes. Each of us is one or the other." The him came over and looked at the large being that had entered his world. He had very large eyes. Tinkle's eyes were large also but not as large as his. When he spoke, his voice was also musical. I suppose in the real world he would have been a baritone. The rhythm of his voice followed some of the lower notes if there were notes in this musical fairyland.

"I would call him Tony, short for baritone. He has a very musical voice that is deeper than yours or mine." Symphony started to sing now as she continued to talk with Tinkle and Tony. It came naturally. Finally, she answered the question Tinkle Bell had asked.

I have not gone to see the Queen. I did not even know you had a queen until you mentioned it. I have never been in such a land as this. It is all new to me. I come from the world above. It is a planet riding out in space. We have countries with different languages but none of our languages are as musical as yours. This is such a beautiful place. Should I go see the Queen? And if so, is she expecting me? To see queens in our world you need an appointment. "They are much too busy to talk to just anyone, especially if that anyone is a stranger to their land like I am." Tinkle thought over the questions before answering. Then the little bell sounds started just as the music score jumped an octave higher.

"The Queen has been expecting you. She knows you are here and told us via the music that if we ran into you to send you to her. She is very interested in why you are here." As the music died away and a new song started, the lonely twin asked for directions.

"I am going that way," chimed in a new Mam or Sir. I will take you right to her door. Do you have a name for me?" As Symphony listened to her voice, she knew this one would need a name that came close to chimes. She could not talk all the time but only when the music demanded it.

"I will call you Chimy. It is a very fitting name for you I believe. What should I expect when I enter the presence of your queen? I would expect she has a name, right?"

"Not really chimed the newcomer. We just call her Queen or Queeny."

Symphony was awakened by the yipping of her new Collie Puppy. He must have awakened from his nap even as she had. His little tummy was probably hungry. Her parents had gotten him for her hoping some company from this sweet little pet would help to ease the loneliness of their distraught daughter. A dark cloud had covered the sun and it appeared the rain that had stopped earlier that afternoon would return. The twin rubbed her eyes and looked at her cell phone. She had been asleep for three hours. Not once during that entire time had she felt sad about the loss of her sister. It had been nice for a change. Perhaps she could come here again when the hurting got so bad and that empty feeling in her soul needed a rest. Mother Vinealeen might take her in her arms once again and rock her to sleep.

CHAPTER 2
Filling the Pain of Loss

In a little while from now
If I'm feeling any less sour
I promise myself to treat myself
And visit a nearby tower
And climbing to the top

Symphony had placed a disk in the keyboard synthesizer and was playing along with her sister Melody. They had recorded each of their parts on separate tracks so if they were ever alone and wanted to do this song, the other twin's part was their waiting. She also had a mic and was singing. The song jumped ahead and continued.

In an effort to
Make it clear to whoever wants to know
what it's like when your shattered
Left standing in the lurch at a church
Where people saying. My God, that's
tough

How she ended up
No point in us remaining
We may as well go home
As I did on my own
Alone again, naturally

And she truly was along again. Another day at school had passed. Another lonely night with no one to share it with except herself. At this point in the song the girls had gone off on a lot of guitar stuff doing runs and things with their instruments. Then she was back at the mic making her own words up if the original ones did not fit.

To think that only yesterday
I was cheerful, bright and gay
Looking forward to who wouldn't do
The role I was about to play
But as if to knock me down
Reality came around
And without so much as a mere touch
cut me into little pieces

The cellphone was ringing. Putting her guitar on the stand she leaned over and picked it up. The name of the person calling sent spine tingling chills down her back. It said that it was Danny. That was impossible! It couldn't be him for he was doing time for vehicular manslaughter. She waited. The call went to voicemail. Someone was recording on the other end. Someone was using his phone. Whoever it was, she wanted nothing to do with anything related to Danny. The lonely twin picked up the guitar and continued singing where the song was.

Why Oh why did she desert me
In my hour of need
I truly am indeed
Alone again naturally
It seems to me that
there are more hearts broken in the
world
that can't be mended
Left unattended
What do we do
What do we do

And what would she do. Turning off the music she decided to hear the voicemail. What came into her ears was bone chilling.

"Melody, Baby. I know you are alive. That wasn't you with me the night of the wreck, it was Symphony. I can swear to it. She was always jealous of what we had. It drove her mad that I chose you. I knew she was tricking me again. You girls were always doing that to me. You were switching places on me. Most people would not have known but you couldn't fool me. I brought your favorite, Wild Turkey Whisky and she wouldn't drink any, not even a drop? That proves it was Symphony right there. She never took a drink after her first one. And when I played your favorite song? She never sang along. You always sang along with that song. I couldn't shut you up. Now I would give anything to hear you sing again and never want you to shut up. There is a giant hole in my heart. You also told me you loved me just before everything went blank. I reached down to kiss you and did not see the stop sign. So, I know you are out there. You can't fool me. I am so sorry about your sister. You know I would never hurt her in a million years. I loved her too. She was part of you, and I had to love all of you. That is the kind of guy I am."

The voice mail was out of space. The phone was ringing again. Symphony tossed it with all her might at the sofa. It hit the back and bounced unto the floor. She went over and stomped on it. Then ran out of the room. She couldn't bear anymore. Not knowing where else to go she headed for the arbor. On the way she saw her dad's hatchet stuck in a stump. She hurled it toward the bottom of the vine before getting into the hammock. Once there she curled up in a little ball and balled. The words of a portion of Alone Again, Naturally came to mind. "And when she passed away, I cried and cried all day, alone again, naturally."

She was inside again. Mother Vinealeen was embracing the girl in her arms again. A few sprinkles of rain filtered through the vines adding tears to the scene. She was at the entrance to the Queen's chambers. True to her word, Chimy had led her right to the very door. She knocked softly and a rich voice called out.

"Who is there?" It was the Queen. Her voice sounded ever so much like a fine-tuned violin. Chimy answered.

"I have brought Symphony to see you just as you asked. She is here with me. Do you want us to come in or is it a bad time?" There was a pause before the Queen answered. It was almost as if she had been crying and wanted to dry her tears.

"Yes, please come in. The door is unlocked." The two entered and their seated on the most beautiful chair Symphony had ever seen sat the Queen. Her eyes were a bit red. Perhaps she had been crying after all. Sympathy went out from Symphony for her. What had happened that would make her so distraught? The queen continued speaking. "They are gone, all of them. The complete south fork was severed. They do not even know it yet. They are still pumping fluid up into the tower, but it is pouring out on the ground. It hurts so bad." She started weeping again and Symphony and the little one by her side chimed in making a trio with tears. When they had finished, the girl noticed the music had stopped. Only the throbbing from way down deep had kept pace with the sobbing. The Queen reached over to a large button in front of her and pushed it. Another song started at her chambers and went out and down, down into the empire below. It was a mournful sounding one. The entire vine started weeping with it. Symphony spoke after it was finished.

"What has happened? Can it be fixed? Surely it can't be as bad as it seems?" The Queen found her voice again.

"How can it be fixed? It has been severed."

"Maybe I can have a look at it? Could someone take me there?" The Queen offered to go with her. They boarded their fastest transportation unit and were at the scene in the blink of an eye. The girl saw where the Queen had been right. It had been severed. She tried to imagine in her mind where it was then remembered the hatchet incident. Her voice came in short, excited gasps as she sang out the words to the Queen. "I will fix it. Don't worry. There has been enough death in the world without something else dying."

Once in the real world she ran to the bathroom and grabbed the first aid kit. Back at the vine Miss Hill united the two pieces together as tight as possible, wrapped them in the cotton gauze and applied the tape. The sap that was flowing all over the ground ceased after a little while. Deep inside the little menders started healing the vine back to normal. For the first time in weeks, Symphony smiled. She had saved a lot of lives today. True, they could never make up for her loss, but it would help. That night she did not cry herself to sleep as before.

CHAPTER 3
Memories

"Hydrotropism is a plants response to water. If there is moisture in the soil, the roots of the plant will gravitate toward it. Moisture has an electrical charge that attracts the cells in the roots of the plants. They can sense it and will send resources down from the upper portion of the plant to aid in reaching it. It is like a magnet. There is one element however that can affect hydrotropism. That is geotropism. Believe it or not plants know about gravity. That is how the tap roots of certain plants go deeper down into the ground. Another aspect that figures into this is how high the plant will grow. The higher it grows, the more the roots need to spread out and down to anchor it into the ground. Please review your notes. There will be a quiz over this material tomorrow." Brown was droning on and on again. Somehow the term quiz registered in the benumbed brain of Symphony but that was all.

She had gone back and listened to the second voice mail from Danny. He really was out. She could not believe it. In some states a person being charged with involuntary manslaughter could spend up to 20 years. What was wrong with Nevada? Why was the penalty so slight? She could still hear his continuing words in her ear.

"Melody, Baby, your killing me. Do you know what kept me going all those long, lonely nights in jail? It was you, Baby. Knowing that you loved me. I dreamt of being in your arms again, holding, you and embracing every part of you. You are so soft. It gives me shivers. Please call me back. If we get together again, I promise I will never drink another drop of that stuff, ever. You will never have to worry about being safe in any vehicle I am driving because I will never get drunk again. Give me one more chance to prove myself, Melody, Sweet. I know how precious you are now. I never valued life like I do now since you, you know what? I love you. I have always loved you and I always will. There is no one else for me. If I can't have you, I won't have anyone. Please! I promise. By the way. If you do not call, I do not know what I will do. I am going crazy lonely, here. I haven't seen you in months. I can't live without you. If I can't have you then I may have to go where Symphony is now, you wouldn't like that, would you?" The phone went blank.

Symphony was madder than she had ever been in her life after that call. Dad had a leather covered boxing ball hooked up at one end of the old chicken coop. There were no chickens now. They had gotten rid of them. After hearing his voice, she took a full-sized photo of Danny out of her sister's stuff and headed for the coop. She taped it to the ball and with her bare fists started pounding away at it. Every time it went away from her and headed back again, she struck again. Ten minutes passed then twenty. In time his face was all battered and bloody. During her fit of anger, she had pounded the skin off some of her knuckles and her blood was mingled with the tattered paper. Danny only had one eye left by the time she was exhausted enough to quit. That was the way Melody had died. One eye had been ripped out of its socket. They had gotten there before she died. It was a miracle but deep inside the sister knew it was her bond to her other half that had kept her alive. Just like the song Melody had been cut into little pieces. The one remaining eye had moved toward her, focusing on her sister and her lips had whispered these parting words.

"I am so sorry I have to leave you, Symph. I love yooo ou, dt don't leave me die alone, hooolld. No n gooodd bys." Her voice had trailed away. Somewhere in the mix of it all Symphony had found her sisters mangled hand and held it until the spark went out of her eye. As the life drained away so did the soul of her survivor. The twin knew she would never be whole again. The part of her that was gone forever was never coming back. So, Alcohol had claimed another life only this time it was not someone else. It was her own flesh and blood.

They found Danny the next morning with so much alcohol in his blood, it was a miracle he could drive at all. He had gotten drunk and gone for a walk looking in every car he could. The first one he found with keys in it he took. They estimated the vehicle hit the concrete buttress at no less than 120 miles per hour. The engine was driven all the way to the back seat. Danny had tried his best to send Symphony on a guilt trip, but she would not have it. It served him right. This girl who had sympathy for a grape vine had no sympathy for her sister's killer. As far as she was concerned, he had committed the unpardonable sin. He had taken her dearest treasure right out of her arms. Symphony did not find comfort in the arms of the mother that afternoon nor even during the upcoming week. Danny's suicide sent her even deeper into that traumatized state she was moving away from. She refused to eat and stayed in bed, skipping school. Her parents were beside themselves as to know what to do. Again, the words of the song came back. What do we do? What do we do? Something had to break the grip her sister's death had on her. That something would come in an unexpected event.

CHAPTER 4
Hit and Run

The little comfort Symph got during that week after Danny's death came from Rexer. There were several times his tiny tongue licked the salt off her tear stained cheeks. She would hold him in her arms close to her heart and talk to him as if he were her long lost sister, clinging to him as she longed to cling to Melody. They had set up a little pen for him in the yard. That was where he could do his business as well as eat and drink. On the morning of the 8th day, she placed him in the pen once more. She walked over to the grape vine to examine the cut to see if it were healing. It was. All the leaves on that vine were alive and doing well. That meant the attempt at grafting she had done, worked. You see this was the portion of the vine that held the Mother's most prized possession. It was the twin grapes way at the top. Since seeing them last Symphony noticed

Mother Vinealeen had added a new leaf over them. Perhaps it was to hide them from the cardinal. When they ripened, many a creature be it bird or squirl would consider them fair game. The entire plant had been pouring its music, heart, and soul into them if a plant has a heart and soul? When the girl returned to the pen however, Rexer was gone. He had dug a hole just big enough to squeeze through and was free.

Symph was beside herself. She looked everywhere for him. Finally, she turned toward the road. She had held off from doing so because if he were there dead also, it would do her in. Coming out from between the Arborvitae trees she saw him. He was halfway across the street. Without looking to the left or right first, she ran toward him. A car driving on the wrong side of the road struck her. She was tossed into the air. There was a sickening thud as she landed on her head and rolled to the side of the road. Rexer hearing the noise turned around from his quest and headed for his mistress. One spot on her head was bleeding. The little puppy started licking it with his tiny, pink tongue. He would alternate between the spot on her head and her face. She never woke up. Her parents found her there with the little one standing guard, fifteen minutes later. The driver never stopped. He or she kept on going. They found a stolen vehicle five miles away wrapped around a telephone pole with what was left of an open bottle of whisky in front. The driver had fled. No one except the puppy saw what happened.

Symphony found herself in the empire of Vinealeen. Melody was there with her or at least to the lonely twin; she wanted it to be her sister. Within the chambers of the empire there were photomere cells that responded to light. They were the communicators and the basis of the music that permeated the place. I suppose from Symphony's standpoint we would need to change the spelling of the word. We will call them photomirror's. About every other place she went these were present, producing a mirror image of the twin. So, it was comforting to the girl to feel she was not the only one of her kind in this place. She could talk with her sister and get a response in one special room. I suppose in this world its counterpart would be labeled a bedroom. It had a bed and whatever items she wanted. In her mind she need only reach for it and it was there. The Mother also communicated with her in this room. She showed her a little door into the future. Symphony could enter it see what would happen in a day, week month or a few years.

It depended on how far she ventured. There were other doors off this special room also. She could go back and relive any experience she ever had. The experience was as real as it can get in a dream state. Today there are millions of people who have lucid dreams. This author has experienced them on several occasions. In the lucid dream state, all the senses are active. One can touch, taste, smell, feel, see, and hear even as if you were there in person. Symph's first trip back in time involved a trip the family took to Disney. The twins were about 12 years old. It was almost perfect.

"What ride do you want to take next, Little Sister?" Melody was giving her the chance to choose this time. Symphony did not know if she liked being called 'Little Sister.' She was only 12 minutes older. Mom had rested for a short time after the older one was born.

"Let's do Splash Mountain," she responded after looking over a board with the map to various attractions. "I heard there are some mines located within 50 miles of our home. It might be fun to see what the mining experience is like." They headed for the roller coaster. During the ride they traveled by river all through the mountain seeing the animated characters acted out on the banks. It was fun. They were seated next to each other when they came to the top of the large fall. They would plunge at tremendous speeds hitting the bottom.

As they had watched others come out soaking wet, they imagined this would be fun. They were supposed to lift their hands up in the air as they plunged downward in that last lap. Symphony and Melody both did that as the camera clicked their picture. The mist in the air sprayed all over them. They were in the portion of the boat that would get the most water. This was fun. At the bottom, the water washed over them. They both screamed as it drenched their clothes. Symph headed over to pick up the photo. She looked and saw herself holding up her hands as the water was washing over her. There was no Melody in the picture. In fact, she was nowhere to be seen. It had been so real. A loud noise interrupted the pleasant experience, and she was back in the room. She exited and headed up to the center of the empire.

"Hello, Symphony," a little voice chimed up. Chimy was there with six new residents. "Do you have names for these?" A light waltz was resounding everywhere. Three of the six trumped a rhythmic run and a door opened. Something was entering the room from the upper portions of the plantation. The twin responded as she watched one of the containers being opened. There were some containers of a gas that was to be released down near the roots. This was a quality check point. One of the Trumpetta's opened a container and the music went an octave higher.

"I will call you 'Trumpetta's,'" the large lady answered. "What do you do here in the empire?"

"In order for the door to open into this room it needs to hear a certain sound. We make that happen." One of the Trumpetta's opened another container. The gas permeated the entire area. It made Symphony sneeze.

"What is that smell?"

"It is CO2," responded another of the Etta's. "This is the lifeblood or our empire. Without it we would die. With it we flourish, and our universe expands." Three of the six figures had been silent during the entire time. They now sounded together as the waltz came to the end of a measure. Another door opened up and a container was brought into the room. Upon opening it, Symph could see what appeared to be white cubes.

"What are these?" She headed over to the container to have a closer look.

"This is sugar. It comes up from the roots. It is the food we eat. You might call the CO2 the air we breathe but this sugar is the food we eat." A Trumputta picked a cube out of the container and gave it to the large person. She put it in her mouth and was very pleased at the flavor. It made her want to sing again. She started humming then responded with a sweet song.

"The three who opened the first door, trumpeting their voices will be called Trumpetta's and the ones who opened up the door on the opposite side of the room, who trumpeted in a lower voice will be called Trumputta's." The six were very pleased. Another, different figure came with a little machine and that made name tags and placed one on each of the six. Trumpetta (1) Trumpetta (2) Trumpetta (3). She then made name tags that read, Trumputta (1) Trumputta (2) Trumputta (3). The little ones went all around the group and with their tiny hands on the tag showing them to everyone. Back in some forgotten corner of her mind Symphony remembered hearing that CO_2 was very bad for the atmosphere. She also in some way realized she was at least consciously inside of the grapevine that grew over the arbor. A question popped into her mind.

"IF CO2 IS THE AIR PLANTS BREATH AND THRIVE IN, WHY WOULD THE POWERS THAT BE WANT TO REMOVE IT FROM THE ATMOSPHERE CUTTING DOWN ON WHAT THEY CALL OUR CARBON FOOTPRINT?"

Would not the end effect of lower amounts of carbon dioxide in the atmosphere harm the world rather than help it? What if they were successful in reducing CO2? Would that not make fewer plants in the world and fewer plants in the world would mean less oxygen? Perhaps the promotion of global warming theories going around were just a scam? Somehow that went against all the supposed facts she had been hearing during her entire educational experience. Next time she was in Biology class she would ask Professor Brown about it. Perhaps it was time for her to make another visit to the Queen. A couple of residents followed her through another door that led to the transportation system. Soon she was at the door.

CHAPTER 5
Sleep Walking

Back in the real world, Symphony appeared to awake from the coma she was in. It had been three days since she had run out in the road after her little puppy. Several people had visited her in thc hospital including the rest of the band. They had gotten special permission to bring their instruments in and play. Nothing seemed to bring her out of her sleep. It was thought that something familiar like her band might activate some memory that would awaken her. They played for an hour and she hardly moved. No medications appeared to work either. It was about 2 am when she sat up in bed, removed the IV from her arm and simply walked out of the building. If any of the staff saw her, they did not attempt to stop her. The hospital was about a fifteen-minute walk from her home. Nobody noticed the door open as she headed for her bedroom. She pulled the covers back and slipped between the sheets. She never heard the phone call from the frantic hospital personal. Her parents never checked her room before rushing back to the building. A search party was called. Several of her friends and band members joined in. They scoured the area around the hospital for the rest of the night with no success. Beside themselves with anxiety, mom and dad returned home with promise of the police department that as soon as any word came in about their daughter a call would come in. It was half by accident and half by habit that mom finally went up to her room and found her sound asleep.

All the authorities were notified, and the doctor came by to check her out. They decided to wake her up so he could examine her. She had struck her head pretty hard. The X-rays showed only a small fracture in her skull, however. She had been fortunate to be alive. Had her head turned even a few inches to the left, she probably would have died. Symphony was fully dressed when they touched her and tried to get her to wake up. She sat up in bed and allowed herself to be examined. Try as they might however, she failed to respond to any outside stimuli. If one were to open her eyes, they would see REM along with occasional NREM going on as her retina appeared to be focusing on something beyond the stimulus. The doctor gave a prognosis of a state of sleep walking where a person's mind is focused on something within the mind while the body goes through the motions of conscious action. After half an hour he left. When it was time for breakfast, Symphony came down all dressed for the day. Anyone who tried to talk to her could not get through. If they tried to stop her movement from place to place, she would stand still until they got out of the way so she could continue doing whatever?

She ate a hearty meal much to the delight of her distraught mother. She also did her normal chores or at least went through the motions. She fed Rexer and spent some time with him as if nothing was wrong. She talked on several occasions. It appeared she was carrying on a conversation with some invisible person. Her words were fully recognizable. Sometimes by listening you could tell she was talking to her twin sister. At other times, it was someone else or several other someone's. Many of conversations did not make much sense. Her mom and dad took off from work for a couple of days to see what would develop. Everyday she followed the same pattern. She got up and dressed, came down for breakfast, played with the puppy for awhile and let him do his thing. Then she would come back to the table for lunch. After lunch she would go to the tool shed, select some pruning shears and a ladder, and spend time cutting away the deadwood from the grape vine. She trained the vines to do different things, go in different directions so they captured maximum light. The entire plant took on an exotic appearance as she worked from day to day. After trimming she would spend some time in the hammock before coming in for the evening meal. After that she would see to the puppy again and retire to her room where she would sit in her sister's favorite chair and stare off into the neverland. She would then shower and retire precisely at 8:30 right to the minute. After the third day of this behavior her parents took turns going to work. Whoever was needed the most got one or the other.

Specialists from all over the nation came to observe her. There had not been many cases of others existing in a state of perpetual sleep walk, so she raised some interest. College students also came who were studying unusual behaviors in people. There were also reporters. She and her sister became quite the celebrities. There story was spread from newspaper to newspaper. A local eyewitness TV station wanted to do a report on her but there was a limit to what the parents would put up with. In time the story leaked to social media. It spread fast causing her to become a social media sensation on several platforms. She developed quite a few fans. Many were urging her to come back from wherever she had gone. Others told her to stay put if she had found happiness and a place where she was not traumatized by loss and pain. Those told her there was enough of that in this world if she had found a land of peace, more power to her. But if she did ever come back to tell others how to go where she had gone if it were indeed her happy place. It all went unnoticed by the twin. She kept up her rituals without fail.

It was time to go see the queen. Symphony made her way to the transportation system and entered. No little insiders accompanied her this time. At the entrance she knocked. A maid fluted to the door and let her in. She had a voice that was higher than the Trumpetta's as she spoke. It followed the rhythms that were wavering in and out of a sound system, piped throughout the entire empire. Something was wrong with the music. The music was really having problems.

"Her Majesty has been expecting you, Symphony. There seems to be more problems springing up. We were so pleased that you could fix the last problem. She will see you now, right this way." Flutissa could not even get around normally. She was hopping and skipping along as she headed toward the queen. Sometimes she would have to hop on one of her tiny legs three times before going to the other one. The little maid escorted her through a hallway and through a couple of doors before turning into a large chamber. Symph had never been in this portion of the queen's residence. It was hard to determine what the room was used for. There were what appeared to be little flags covering one room. The queen was in a mobile throne. She turned when the musician entered and addressed her.

"Greetings to you Symphony. I have been meaning to ask how you have been doing since we last met. I was worried when word came to us that you had been struck by a drunk driver out there. We could feel your pain. How is your head feeling? I understand you were thrown up in the air and came down on it pretty hard." The twin responded after racking her brain to try and remember anything about the accident. She was going across the road after Rexer and then everything went blank. Next, she remembered being in the empire of Vinealeen. The ancient mother had soothed her fears. She could sense her now running her ancient hands through her hair, she examined the wound. Symphony was struggling with some forgotten thing. She felt a warm sensation cleaning the blood away. But she could not see who was doing that.

"I think I am feeling fine now. I do not have any headaches anyway. It only hurts if I place my fingers up there and press down. Then a pain will start at the point of contact and shoot all the way down my spine. I can feel it in my toes if I press too hard. Thanks for asking."

"You are most welcome. Thanks for putting the empire back together after part of it was severed. Nobody saw what happened." Symphony knew. During a fit of anger, she had hurled the ax at the vine and the blades had done the rest. She wondered if she should confess. A little voice inside of her said no. Some things were best left unconfessed. "We have some more problems going on. There are some foreigners that are trying to enter our boarders. They are breaking through a portion of them at three places. I will show you the locations." Queeny pulled out a map and pointed out the areas. Symphony could somehow interpret this map. In her mind she saw three areas up there where carpenter ants were chewing through some old dead portions of the vine. At their current rate, they would be inside within a couple of days. That would cause some of the precious fluid that kept everything flowing to be lost. She would need to go to the shed and get some pruning shears and cut them off back to the vine. Then she would spray some black pruning paint over the cut. No ants would bother again. They did not like that black stuff at all.

"I will get right on it. I think it is causing the music to sound offbeat.   If your music gets messed up much more, it could be disastrous for the health of this place."

"That is what I admire about you. When we heard your name, we knew that you were the one to bring us back from the brink of destruction. Back in the earliest days of our existence we produced so much fruit. People came from all over to partake with us. We had bountiful harvest year after year. Then the outside environment started crowding in all around us. It became harder to breath and our music was very nearly extinguished. Now we have hope again. There is someone here who can help us and fix things up that need repair. A very musical someone might I add." The musician did not feel much like that this evening.

"I would like you to come with me. There are some things I want you to know about since you will be a permanent resident here for the next few weeks," the queen continued speaking as her hoverchair started to move toward a large, double door. The queen and the chair easily fit inside. This was the grandest transportation system in the entire place. In no time they were up to the top of Vinealeen. The doors opened out into a beautiful green room. It was like passing into a room of emeralds. The sun was shining brightly outside and as the rays entered the room, there were little notes dancing around. There were thousands of them. They were far smaller than the residents such as Flutissa and Tinklebell. They would grab a ray of sunshine and swallow it. Then the notes would start to dance and convert the sunbeam to music. The music was then taken to capsules that once full would be loaded into small holes in a wall on one side of the room. The Notelings were not large enough to put them into the holes so there were several residents that looked like Obos. They made the most unusual sound as they worked with the rhythm of the music. One of them came over to Symphony and asked her a question.

"We have heard that you are naming all the residents in Vinealeen. What name would you give us?" Several of them in concert went through a run of notes that first went up the scale then down. Each sang a different note and it blended wonderfully like a sextet was doing it. Every note was perfectly pitched. Then they started to join in with the music that was going throughout the entire empire. It was so very unique. No sound was like this out there, or if it were, the musician had never heard the like. She wracked her brain. It did not seem to be working right today somehow. But forgetting about that something popped into her mind.

"I think there is a name that suits you very nicely. Obosaleen." You are the Obosaleens of the empire of Vinealeen. The is where all the beautiful music starts. From here it is piped all throughout the empire. "Without you, Obossaleens, the music in this place would be much less effective in causing the residents to properly do their work." The Obosaleens were extremely pleased with their new name and started repeating it every time they placed a green capsule in one of the holes. Even the Notelings were pleased and started to work faster. Symphony glanced at the queen. A beautiful ray of green light was seeping through a lens in the ceiling. She was bathed in a yellow-green robe of splendor that made all of the little diamonds in her dress sparkle. She was smiling.

After receiving her bath in the light, the queen exited the green room and entered another transportation chamber. It went even higher into the heavens. There was a beautiful window that looked out over the yard. Symphony could see her house. She could see the little pen the puppy was placed in when he was not being watched. A door opened and her mother came out and sat down on a chair on the porch. She was looking off to the mountains on her right. for a brief moment she glanced directly at her daughter. Large tears were streaming freely down her face. She was weeping uncontrollably. It was something Symphony would remember long after this day passed. She had never seen her mother shed a tear. What was troubling her? She wanted to run to her and throw her arms around the distraught woman and comfort her. That would make both of them feel better. The daughter wondered why she had never bonded with her mom. She was a very beautiful woman and looked like an older version of the twins. They all had those steelier features that propelled them into the best of the best-looking women in society. Any handsome man would be proud to have her any of them on his arm as he went anywhere in public. It is not that her mom had not tried to communicate with the girls, she had done her best to instill in them morals that would rise them above the average riffraff of girls that plagued society. She had not been successful in passing those morals on to Melody though. Symphony had adopted them for the most part. She did not go out and make a fool of herself with the guys. She was not promiscuous in any way. No guy, however good looking was going to paw her all over. Her body was off limits for roaming hands and feeling fingers.

Above the queen and her guest were the twin grapes hanging there off the veranda. They were just starting to color a little. The green was blushing. Shades of red started at the stem and made little streamers of color that went all the way down to the bottom of the fruit. They were very beautiful. Symphony was amazed at how large they were in comparison to her and the queen. For the first time since entering Vinealeen, she wondered how someone nearly as large as her mother out there could be miniaturized enough to enter into the daily life of the residents of this empire. It was then a moment of realization hit her. She had come within to escape something out there, something that was too dark and sinister for her to handle at this time. Everything she was witnessing now was not reality. It was all make believe. This came as a great relief to her. She could be anything she wanted to be in this world. She could shed all her pretenses and finally be herself. Since nothing was real no one could or would judge her on any of her actions in here. She was free at last. She started to sing a beautiful song that made its way throughout the entire empire of Vinealeen. It was:

THE SONG OF THE GRAPE

The sun is shining brightly
on the land of Vinealeen.
Like a million, tiny raindrops
from the sea.
And all the world is singing
in this land of Vinealeen.
Within it's like a beautiful,
wonderful dream.
Look at the tiny grapes, see how their growing.
Here in this land of bliss, their colors showing.

I wish the world could enter

this land of Vinealeen.
Where the music plays all day
throughout the land.
And everyone stays busy
in this land of Vinealeen.
As they tend the grapes that
come forth from their hand.
Someday you'll pick the fruit when it matures.
And taste its marvelous juice when that occurs.

Even the fruit is singing in
the land of Vinealeen.
As it swells in size its colors can be seen.
Their song is one of gladness
in this land of Vinealeen.
They are joined by all for
every one of them beams.
Look at the tiny grapes, see how their growing.
Here in this land of bliss, their colors showing.

There is one verse to go
from this song of Vinealeen.
It's the saddest verse the
grapes will ever know.
For some would spoil the
music of this land of Vinealeen.
They ferment the juice this
wonderful empire grows.
Look at the many grapes, now that their gotten.
They added other stuff, to make them rotten.

Symphony never intended to end the song that way when she started but as the memory of her sister came to mind, she once again became sad. It was fermented juice after all that had ripped her heart out on that dark, dark night. While she was singing the rhythm of the entire vine changed its song and joined in. The trumpets were trumpeting, while the oboes were oboeing. The chimes were chiming in tune as the rest all joined in. Deep in the roots the drums were sounding out the beats. For a few brief moments the musician and the vine were one and the same. And was it not a true story? Why were most of the grapes produced in the nation? To be fermented and drunk by the entire population. It was a sad but true ending to a great start for the song. Symphony found herself at the supper table. Mom and dad were there with her. They had started making this meal a permanent part of their day. It was a time for them to be with their estranged daughter one more time before she followed her routine of going off to bed. Tonight, they received the surprise of their lives though for their daughter started talking. This was the first time she had spoken to them in weeks. Meanwhile, Symphony, still believing this entire ritual was part of her hide-a-way world of make-believe, decided she could say whatever was on her heart to her parents because, in reality, it was not actually happening.

Perhaps at this point in the story, let's say you are a young person. You have never been able to freely communicate with your parents or guardians. It would be like living a nightmare to tell them everything that you are thinking about. Suppose you have been doing some things that they would not approve of and were they to know the truth of it, they would give you the tongue lashing of your life, cussing you up one side and down the other, maybe even kicking you out of the house. Now suppose you felt your guardians were not real but make-believe. That it all was a dream. That once you talked things out, told them everything, got it off your chest, you would wake up in the morning and nobody would ever know the difference. Now, place yourself in the shoes of

Symphony. She does not believe her parents at the table across from her will ever hear what is on her mind and what she is about to say because it is all a bad dream, and in the morning will be over. The people listening to her are not really there in person. To have an open dialogue like that between kids and their parents is rare indeed in this world we live in today. Communication is never complete, never. That is unless...

CHAPTER 6
Confessions of the Heart

Now where were we? Oh, I remember, we were at the supper table. Symphony was about to start talking because though she realized she was alive, she somehow felt everything she was experiencing was a dream and would one day be over.

"Mom, Dad, there are some things I need to tell you. I know you will not get mad because, well because we all know what is happening here. It started a long time ago, Melody's drinking and drug using. I am sure you know about both, but perhaps not the entire truth of it. Danny introduced us to beer on our thirteenth birthday. He brought over three bottles. His dad of course was an alcoholic and owns a liquor store so, he had easy access to the stuff. From the moment I tasted it, I knew I would never develop a liking for it. Melody said I made a terrible taste and started to pour the stuff out on the grass, but Danny stopped me. He said if I were going to dump it out, he would drink it. He hadn't opened his bottle yet, so he took mine and drank it. Melody did not like it either at first but, she was not going to give up. She stuck it out and got it all down. Later she threw most of it up as her stomach revolted. But every time he would bring some around, she would do it again. Soon he started bringing the real hard stuff. I would usually go away and let them do their thing together.

After drinking, Danny would start petting her, feeling her all over with his hands and trying to kiss her. It took awhile but soon she joined in and they thought it was funny to make out in front of me because I made such a fuss about it. You see, my sister and I are only half a person by ourselves. I know what she is feeling, and she knows what I am feeling unless she is under the influence. I felt the first time they had sex. It was like it was being done to me. I was being raped though because I did not want it to happen. So, for me it was a forced thing. I started hating Danny then. He figured it out after a while." Mom turned a bit sheepish over Symphony's bold description. She turned a few shades of color lighter as some of the blood drained from her face, then she spoke.

"How old were you and your sister when, you know, when he did this to you?" Without even blinking the twin answered.

"It was about two months before our 14th birthday." Dad was the one to be surprised this time. Only rather than turning white, he started to turn red as the anger begin to raise within him. He controlled it a little before he spoke.

"Did you see it happen? Did he do it in front of you?"

"No, when he started pawing her all over, I left disgusted. Melody was egging him on. I could feel her heart racing as he got closer to her private part down there. When his cold fingers touched it, I shrieked. I thought you might have heard me. I was in my room by the time he did that. He dragged an old mattress in from the pile of stuff that you had slated for the dump. When she got in later that night, she felt dirty all over. She stayed in the shower for over half an hour. Then, an hour later took another shower. We always talked about everything but that night she was silent. I can read her thoughts though at times, closer to the time she drifts off to sleep. I can tune in. She was ashamed and humiliated. Her privacy was forever gone. And I hated Danny even more for hurting her like that. For the first time in my life, I wanted to kill somebody, I wanted him dead, and you know I have a kind heart." Dad knew that feeling this very moment, at least the thought of wanting to hurt someone real bad, anyway. As the thought of his beloved daughter being pawed all over at 13 years of age? The blood started to raise again up to his face. He excused himself.

"I have to go and do something. It will not take long. I will be back in 5 or 6 minutes." He left in a real hurry. Symphony and her mom heard some things banging around outside. He had to get this out of his system, or he would do or say something he would later regret. Mom chimed in with a statement. They had finished the main part of the meal although everyone had food left on their plate.

"I am going to the freezer to grab some Ice Cream Sandwiches for each of us. Don't you think it is pretty warm in here? The ice cream will cool us down." Symphony took advantage of the time to run up to her room and grab some photos. Soon they were all back at the table eating the ice cream. Everyone was strangely quiet. Finally, the girl continued telling her story.

"By the time Mel was 14, she and Danny were smoking marijuana on a regular basis. By then sex was like putting on a pair of comfortable blue jeans only in her case, they were coming off. Before we turned 15, they had tried every drug they could get their hands on. Danny started to steal money from his dad. Then when that was not enough, he did the worst thing I never thought he could possibly do. He told her to start chipping in or he was going to break up with her. Then he said he had talked with the Fenton kid. His dad is a banker, you know. He had a big pocketbook. He told Melody to make out with him for money." Mom gasp, got up from her chair and ran to the door. The contents of her stomach spilled out in the yard. Dad brought his fist down on the table so hard, three dishes partially filled with food, clattered to the floor spilling their contents all over it. Symphony, knowing this was all a dream, watched. When they returned she spoke very calmly. She had been about to show them some photos of her sister and Danny with their arm all tightened up ready for the needle but stopped and hid them behind her back.

"I can see that everyone is getting a little hot under the collar so we will continue this discussion tomorrow evening after it soaks in, that is unless I wake up by then of course at which point you will never hear another word about this from me." She left them speechless, sitting at the table looking at each other with a look she had never seen on their faces before. Something came up the following night though. They did not even gather around the table but grabbed something and made it look like they were very busy. This happened for the next week. All this time Symphony remained in her sleep walk state, waiting. If was Friday evening before they were gathered once more around the table. She brought the pictures out right away.

"Here is your daughter and that, that thing doing this. I want you to see that I am telling the truth. I may be dreaming but this story is real." Mom and dad picked up the photos. Melody had dark circles around her eyes. She looked exhausted in the first photo. The second one showed her flinching a bit as the needle penetrated her skin. Then she was removing the strap in the next one. In a final photo, she looked relaxed and happy. There was a smile on her face as the drugs started to take effect. Symphony started to show the next ones but thought better of it and drew back. They would never see these photos.

"The night of the automobile accident I pleaded with Melody to resist drinking just this once. They had already had their refer so were relaxed. She laughed at me. It was then I did something I wish I had not done. I hauled off and punched her as hard as I could. 'I am not joking with you sister. I am as serious as I can be. You have gone way to deep into this. You will do what I say, or I am going to tell Mom and Dad every little detail of your double life. Do you understand?' I punched her one more time. Danny saw me do it. He saw her double over as my fist landed in her gut. He came running over like he was going to plough me over. I stepped back, raised my leg and he went flying into the dirt. I went up and kicked him in the side. I told him if he didn't stop killing my sister with this stuff, I would see that he never hurt her again. He had turned to face me and just to get my point across, I kicked him as hard as I could where it would hurt him the most. Melody had recovered by then and came at me from the side. She was too much under the influence though and I sidestepped her. She landed on Danny who was using every foul word he could think of. Then, it was over. The funniest thing happened. The reefer must have finally hit its full effect. They started to laugh. They must have laughed for five minutes rolling around on the ground in hysteria before they left. 'That was a good one, Symphony, you really got us. Way to go girl, way to go, groovy' Then they went to his car and drove off. That was the last I saw her before in the car, you know. I never got a chance to say I am sorry to her." Mom and Dad got up from the table and came over to her side. She was crying. Both of them placed their arms around her and cried with her. And with that crying, healing came. For Symphony it was as if a giant burden had been lifted off her shoulder.

The following day after going through her rituals, she went once again to the hammock and stretched herself out under the ancient vine. It was in pristine condition by now. The carpenter ants had been taken care of. Every little dead stem from the vine had been pruned off and pruning paint applied. The two grapes at the top were red now. Soon they would start to darken to a deep violet before that deep blue color that Concords are noted for came.

She was inside the vine. She made her way to a room she had never been to before. I suppose in our world it would be the equivalent to the theater.

Several of the residents from the empire of Vinealeen were gathered there watching a movie. There was this big tree of fruit. Under it were gathered all kinds of African animals. There were elephants, baboons, monkeys, several types of grazers and even some hyenas. The fruit had fallen to the ground and was fermenting. As the animals ate it, they started to get drunk. The elephants had eaten so much, they could not walk straight. One of them even fell over. The monkeys were doing crazy things, running round and round in circles. The grazing animals were rocking back and forth not knowing what they were doing. As the residents watched, they would fall down and roll around on the floor with laughter. Symphony had never seen them with such merriment before. It was a new insight into their life she had not been a part of before. After a time, she left.

Mother Vinealeen had given her a special room where she could hang out and do whatever she liked. It was the room that had doors going off in different directions. She chose one she had never been through before. Inside there were several windows. As she traveled along a hall way looking through the windows, she came to one that had her sister in it. Symphony could not believe what she saw. Melody was pregnant. She also looked older, like she might be 18 or 20. It was hard to tell as the extended use of the drugs had prematurely aged her. She must have been eight months along because she was big. There was a little nook Symphony could fit in. She settled herself down and watched. Danny came in and started yelling at her sister. He was very drunk. Then he hauled off and struck her in the eye. When she started to cry, he pushed her to the ground and started kicking her. Finally, his foot came over to her stomach. The poor girl had tried to protect her baby. Both hands were there when the shoe hit. It broke three of her fingers. He left her curled up in a ball crying. She fast forwarded to the hospital. The baby was being born. Danny was there all sober this time.

　　　　She saw the doctor come out and talk to her parents. He was shaking his head. The baby was still born. Danny had killed it with that kick. Symphony saw another button and touched it. Sound came. She watched as Danny was approaching Melody. He was crying.

"Baby, Baby. I am so sorry. I promise I will never touch that stuff again, you will see." The twin went ahead in time. She was spinning through the motion now. She saw this beast beat up her sister time and again. Apologizing each time that it would be the last and her sister believing it, always returning to him for more. Finally, as this look into the future of a life her sister would have lived had she not died in the accident,

Symphony saw him kill her in cold blood. He beat her until her body was hardly recognizable. Then he stomped out of the house. The police arrested him a few hours later.

She was able to see the reaction her parents had at this other death, had their daughter lived on for a few more years. They were broken. She watched them fight more and more until they separated and finally divorced. She could see herself and the effect all of this had on her as a person. Finally, she knew. She understood why it had happened. Her sister would have married that beast and he would have killed her with his own hands. The emotionally tired guest to Vinealeen drifted off into a deep sleep. When she woke up, she was in the real world again. Only this time, she knew. Inside she knew that though what had happened had been a great trauma to her, had it not ended that way, her sister would have had to live in hell with that devil of a man for five years.

CHAPTER 7
A Choice: Love or Friendship?

Symphony was a different person now. She finished out the year at high school and got the band back together again. As the end of her nightmare story finally came to social media, her fan base seemed to grow. Money started to come in. People started programs in their community on alcohol and drug awareness. She would get reports from kids who had turned away from that kind of life because of what had happened to her. When the ladies band played, there were several newcomers who stopped by. The band wanted to do a tribute song for Melody, but the creative juices of the entire group had dried up. They stuck with popular hard rock songs when they played. They did them well. That summer several trips were taken to nearby cities. Money started to come in so the band members could invest in better equipment. A local production company had them do a CD. On the cover was a favorite photo of Symphony's. It was her and her sister rocking out doing their thing.

All the time however, Symphony kept asking herself what she wanted to do with her life. College was coming up. Should she go? Her grades had suffered during her time of trouble. The GPA she needed for entrance into some colleges was not there. in the meantime, she and the band kept going. The schedule started to fill up every weekend for them. Perhaps a music career would be in her future. She could only wonder. One day during down time, she went once more to the hammock and drifted off into a light sleep. She was inside again greeting all her old friends. The grapes were about ready to harvest. Vinealeen was singing their best. It was the queen who finally brought some sense to the wandering spirit of this sole surviving twin.

"It has been quite awhile since you visited us, Symphony. The entire empire has missed you. It was like you up and left us once you fixed all our music problems. What have you been doing with yourself these last several weeks? We can see so little from here. You come and go, and the band comes and practices in the building but that is about all we know. Of course, Mother Vinealeen knows your every move. When we ask her about you, she has that ancient smile of wisdom that comes over her wrinkled brow. The wrinkles all turn up and look happy. Then she says she is working on something. It was different the other day though. She stated you would be coming home. She told me to tell you to come here Saturday afternoon exactly at three. You are to pick the two grapes. She said for you to bring a paper towel with you. Then you are to join us in here. The entire empire will be here. This will be a great celebration for all of us. This is the first harvest we have had in years. You see, you are to eat the grapes, all except the seeds. You are to wrap the seeds in the paper towel and let them sit for exactly 30 days. That before those days are up, if you have eaten the grapes and joined us, and done everything she has ask, that a miracle will happen that will change your life forever. Do you have any idea of what is up with this?" Symph had to think long and hard. They were scheduled to play in a park for a family reunion three cities over. Three O-Clock would be right in the middle of their performance.

"I am with the band then doing entertainment for a family reunion. Their son who saw my story is home for a couple of weeks from his duty with the military. He asked them to get our band. He said he was my biggest fan. How can I be in two places at once?"

"Mother stated that would be the case, she said you would have to decide. On the one hand you meet this guy and his family, on the other you join all of us in this empire wide celebration of harvest. It is a tough decision. She told me to tell you to choose wisely." Symphony was struggling. Had it not been for this empire that took her in during her dark night, she would not be this far on her way to recovery. She thought back over the last several weeks and tried to decide. She could not.

"I will have to think it over, Your Majesty. This is a big opportunity for us. His parents said they have contacts." The Queen thought her answer over then responded.

"How do you feel when you are performing, leading out in the songs with your guitar in hand. Is your heart and soul in it?"

"Now that you put it that way, no. I am just passing time, going through the motions and from what I hear, those motions are very good. People like me, they like us, we are getting noticed more and more, but no. My heart is not really in it. Half of me is out there wandering in the autumn mist doing something with Puff the Magic Dragon in a land called Honah Lee."

"Do you trust us? Do you trust Mother Vinealeen?"

"Yes, very much."

"Can she work miracles?"

"I believe with all of my heart that she can make anything happen. When I first entered your empire, she gave me a chance to totally relive some of the good times I had with Melody while we were still innocent and happy. It was the happiest I had been since she died."

"Then trust her one more time. She said if you do not, one of the grapes will be spoiled. To keep it from happening, you need to be here precisely at three. If you are even a minute late, it will be forever too late. Your fate will be set. I could see in her ancient eyes that this is serious."

"I will try to make it, My Queen. I will talk it over with the band members and see what we decide." She was about to go when looking into the violet eyes of the Queen one last time she heard her whisper: *"Please, don't let us down. Everyone will be so disappointed if you do not come."*

The week passed quickly. The girls would be doing a new song. It was quite popular now, climbing up the charts. Friday evening before her big day Symphony chanced to look out at the grape vine. The last rays of the sitting sun were shining on the two ripe grapes at the top. They showed deep blue, even deeper than the blue skies in the east while the leaves were bathed in a golden light. It was a beautiful sight. She found herself going out there and sitting one more time in the hammock. She had decided to go with the band to the reunion but wanted to say goodbye in her own silent way. As she rocked back and forth, there was a deathly silence. She could no longer feel the empire. It was gone. She tried. She talked to them. She did some meditations to try and get herself in the mood, but all was as still as death. Her soul was wrenched one more time. Had they too abandoned her? Inside she laid out her clothes for the following day. They would need to leave by ten in the morning to make it to the reunion and get set up before the celebration. After several hours, she dropped off into a troubled sleep.

The next morning, she decided she would take her own car. It was actually Melody's though. It had not been driven since her death. Once in awhile she would go and start it up and back it in and out of the garage but that was about it. The other band members would take the van with the equipment. At the park everything was decorated perfectly. The parents had spared no expense to make his homecoming reunion the best it could be. When Symphony met him, her heart did a few skips. He was all man. His smile was like the blue sky on a cool summer morning. He was easy to talk to. He appeared to idolize her, watching her every move. And when she sang, one pair of blue eyes never left her face. It inspired her like nothing had in a long time. The old spark started to come back. They did three songs and took a break. It was during that break she chanced to look at her watch. It was one O'Clock. She still had time to make it back home if she left now. He was coming toward her with the broadest smile she had ever seen. When he got close, she raised up on her tip toes and whispered in his ear.

"Do you believe in miracles, Adam?"

"Yes, I do, Symphony.   I am experiencing one right now."

"If you had one chance to be a part of a miracle, would you take it?"

"I would not hesitate, Symph. I would do it regardless of what others might think. I would go all in and never look back unless looking back was a good thing."

"Then I must do this one thing, Adam.   I must leave now. I have thousands of little ones depending on me, hoping against hope that I will be there. I cannot let them down. I have enjoyed meeting you and your invitation to our band was wonderful! You and your family are the greatest. You won't hold it against me for leaving right in the middle of this will you?"

"If you know deep, down in your heart you must do this, then go. Do not disappoint those thousands of little ones. They are more important than just one of me. I do not want to be selfish. I will share you with them if it is as important as you say." Upon hearing his response, she reached up and gave him a sweet kiss on his cheek. Then she was running to her car.

On the way back to Vinealeen, she was speeding a little too fast. When the lights came on, she groaned. If this took even five minutes, she would not make it. The clock was ticking. When the officer came up to the car, she had her license and registration ready. Then the grandest words came out of his mouth.

"You are Symphony, aren't you? I have been following your story. You are a survivor. I will give you credit for that. It takes a lot to come out of what you came out of. My son was killed in an alcohol related accident. I do not need to see your license. I know who you are. Why are you in such a hurry?"

"The people who got me through my sleep walk are waiting for me back home. If I do not make it by three, they will be so disappointed, and I think I will be too."

"Well, if they helped you then I will help you now, that is if you want me to. Could you use a police escort?"

"Officer. You are the best. Yes, Yes. What is a police escort might I ask?"

"Let's put it this way. If you need to drive a little faster, no other officer will stop you if they see me behind you with flashing lights. People will pull over to the side of the road for you and me as we pass. You will save a good seven minutes." He looked at his watch and nodded before continuing. "Yes, seven minutes, I think that will get you to your house about 5 minutes before three. Are you ready to go? Instead of driving 50, go 70 mph. I will be right behind you and please, drive carefully!"

She was off with the lights flashing behind. She made it home in record time. She was pulling into her driveway at 7 minutes to three. He saluted her as he continued on. She had just enough time to go in and gather the paper towel, pull the ladder out of the shed, and set it up. At exactly 2 minutes to 3 she picked the two grapes and was in the hammock 30 seconds early.

Symphony found herself in the empire of Vinealeen. Everyone was there dressed in their Saturday best. They were all so happy. Then the ancient lady herself came. She was dressed in her royal robes with a golden crown on her head. The entire empire bowed when she entered. She was ready to start the ceremony. Symphony had made the right choice. A miracle would happen. A hush fell over the throng as the ancient one started to talk.

"Citizens of Vinealeen. This is a very happy day indeed. It is a day of change. Wonderful things will be coming to this empire. And a miraculous change will come to Symphony. We have struggled with her through this great loss. Half of her heart was ripped from her chest with the lost of her dearest friend on earth, her sister, Melody. Though she can not be with us today, her spirit is among is. We can feel her with us. She has been as much a part of this time of change as has Symphony. Now the time has come to plant the seeds of a miracle, a miracle that will ring down through our ages as a great moment in time. And for Symphony, she does not know what is about to happen. But she fulfilled her part of the agreement so we will fulfill ours. Symphony, as she eats these grapes that we have put so much of our time and effort into, will be the recipient of something wonderful! She will not know when it will happen. But it will. Before the next thirty days are up, she will have witnessed a miracle. Not only witness it but be a recipient of it. It will bless her in ways that she cannot now comprehend. The time for change in her life and ours has come. Today it starts. Let the celebrations begin." There was a moment of stillness as the ancient lady looked out over the crowd.

She seemed to peer into each set of eyes looking back at her then continued. She now addressed the twin.

"First, Symphony, you must eat the grapes, all but the seeds. The inside will be very sweet. The peeling though will be very sour. You must eat the sour with the sweet, every drop, every bit. Once it is gone, place the seeds in the paper towel and let them sit for 30 days exactly. You will then plant them in clay pots at exactly 3 in the afternoon thirty days from now. Are you ready?"

Symphony looked at the two grapes in her hand. They did look good. She could smell the sweet scent of them. It came wafting up, entering her nose and teasing her taste buds. She could not recall ever eating a Concord Grape before. All the ones she had eaten were from the store and seedless. There had been green, red and dark purple ones. Their skin had been crispy. She wondered why the skin of these would be sour or bitter. It did not make sense. She looked at the ancient matriarch. The wise one spoke again.

"Symphony, life is like these two Concord Grapes you hold in your hand. There are times when on the outside, life throws you its toughest curve ball, a ball that corves so fast it comes and hits you in the gut. You double over as you are hit. It hurts like nothing you have ever experienced before. These are the hard times that come to all of us. Everyone experiences them. But for each hardship in life, there are the sweeter times that follow, times so sweet that the sour is forgotten. This my beloved Symphony is the song of the Concord, the true song of the grape. It is time for you to eat them. You may choose which ever one you like to eat first but you must eat them one at a time."

The twin looked at both grapes then without taking too long to decide popped the one in her right hand into her mouth. As her teeth sank into it the rich, sweet juice spilled out into her mouth. It was divine. It was like heaven had plucked its most choice fruit and given it to the young lady. She savored each droplet of nectar. She separated the seeds from the gel and carefully placed them in the folded paper towel. It had been wonderful! Then the peeling gave her all it had of sour. After the sweetest of the sweet it was brutal tasting. She wanted to spit it out. In fact, she did put it in the hand where she had taken it from as she made a sour face. She looked at it there, empty and broken with its gaping hole. That had been her just a few weeks ago. She had been this grape peeling. All empty and broken with all the goodness squeezed out of her. But the instructions were to eat all except the seeds. She must take the bitter with the sweet, so she put it back in her mouth and chewed it up into tiny bits. As that happened, the peeling grew sweeter and sweeter. Though it was not as sweet as the inside of the grape she could tolerate it.

As she swallowed the last of it, the entire population of the empire were cheering. A great cry of joy went up. There was one grape to go. This time she separated the inside from the peeling in her mouth, chewed up the bitter peeling first and swallowed it before indulging her taste buds with the sweet, juicy nectar. It was worth the wait. At last, the seeds came out and were placed with the others in the paper towel. It was done. She had made it! The celebration lasted for two hours after. One hour for each grape. Symphony had finally found peace.

CHAPTER 8
AN AMERICAN IDOL

A week passed and then two. Symphony and her band played four times. Adam managed to make it to one performance. He appeared to be the perfect gentleman. They went out and shared a meal at a restaurant. It was the day before he had to return to duty. At seventeen, Symphony was not ready to enter into a relationship with any guy, still it was a welcomed change to match wits with someone from the other side. It was apparent that this was not the miracle Mother Vinealeen was referring to. She checked the seeds wrapped tightly in the paper towel every now and again. Something was happening within them during this time. She tried to recall if her Biology teacher, old professor Brown had discussed anything about this but could not recall ever a mention of it. Rexer was growing quite quickly now and was fast becoming too large to be a lap dog although he did not understand that but still tried to crowd himself unto her lap. From time to time the wondering teenager would spend a few moments in the hammock just incase there was any word from this empire. There was not. Perhaps she wondered if since her need was less, their attention to her was diminished. Would she ever be able to go back and visit all her friends there, if so, would there be changes? Plants went through a lot of changes in preparation for winter. It might have been nice to be a part of them but alas, this was not to be.

One evening since there was a lull in her schedule, Symph decided to watch some television. During her time of duress, she had not focused much on this. She did not have any special programs she liked to watch in particular so, was flipping channels. She chanced on a rerun from American Idol. She saw thousands of young people lined up to test out their voices with the judges. There was a screening process going on. A young man was trying to impress the screeners with his master of the art, but they were not impressed. Neither was she. In the entire song he had tried to memorize, I say tried for he was not even successful at that, he could not remember the words so was making some up as he went. She was about to switch the channel when there staring back at her was the next contestant. She could not believe her eyes. She was the spitting image of Melody and herself. Her face was a near exact match. Her nose, mouth face body size, everything was cut from the same mold as the twins. There was one different thing about her, no, two. Ratner than blond, her hair was brown. And rather than the blue jeans the girls chose to wear, she was wearing a dress. It was a longer one, it went down past her knees and was not stylish at all. Symphony waited breathless as she started to sing. It was at that moment the twin realized something nearly impossible. Her voice was an exact match of her late sister's. She did a stellar performance with her selection, not unlike the former contestant. She hit every note, her timing was right on. There was not even a hint of a flaw during the entire time. She was placed in a line that would actually be broadcast as she went before the judges to convince them she was capable of being the next American Idol.

Symph had remembered to hit the record button with the remote. It had a feature that allowed the viewer to send a portion of the program to memory. It could hold up to four hours. You could program it to record your favorite show if you were not going to be home, even have it remove the advertisements if you so desired. She had to show her parents this one. They would probably be as amazed as she had been. The girl went by the name of Rapsody. As the minutes counted down to her stage performance, the camera focused on others who were in the line. She shut the record feature off for this. When the time came for her to do her thing, she bounded up the stairs to the stage. The judges asked her the normal questions. Finally, the last one came.

"Why do you want to be the next American Idol?" Rapsody got the sweetest smile on her face, she looked off toward the ceiling for a moment before responding.

"My parents and sister are watching me from up there. They were killed in an automobile accident nine months ago. This was my dream as well as theirs. We watched every one of your shows. Deep inside we knew this was my destiny. So, this song is for them and especially for my Mom."

"And what song will you be singing for them."

"Coat of Many Colors." There was an understanding nod from the judges as she gave the title. Though she did not have a coat of many colors, stitched together from a box of rags, her dress was an example that she had not come from a family that had a lot of money. And so, she started singing. She hit every note, the first part of the song was perfect. She did it better than Dolly Parton. The entire group of people listening in the audience as well as around the world on television were into it. She had captured them until. Symphony watched with remorse when Rapsody, faltered on one verse and started to cry sing. She had gotten to the part of the song that spoke of her momma blessing the coat with a kiss.

"And I just couldn't wait to wear it,
And momma blessed it with a kiss.

She was crying now as the tears streamed down her face, but she recovered and continued.

So with patches on my britches
And holes in both my shoes
In that coat of many colors
I hurried off to school."

And so, it was over. One judge jumped to her feet. Half of the people in the audience were standing. A chant had started. The one standing judge tried with all her persuasive power to get the others to stand with her but they would not. She had messed up. Suppose she were up in front of ten thousand fans and made a mistake like that? It was with great disappointment the girl-crying once again-left the stage. Symphony was heart stricken for her. She had entered fully into her story, her performance. Like with her sister, even though this was a re-run, she had felt the pain deep in her gut. Though this was not Melody, it was her spirit up there longing to be recognized.

The twin listened as she spoke of her disappointment to the camera crew after it was all over. She gave the town where she was staying. It was about a two-hour drive. After losing her parents, her aunt had reluctantly taken her in. There was nowhere else for her to go. Her aunt was very conservative and had her distinct view of how a lady should look and dress. Rapsody did not say if her parents shared these same views. She had saved her money for months to make the trip. Unlike her parents, her aunt was totally against this nonsense. They had finally come to a plea bargain agreement. Her aunt would let her go but if she were rejected, this nonsense she and her parents had would never be brought up again. It was tough but the girl was confident she would make it. Now she had failed and walked away broken. Her dreams had been totally shattered.

Symphony stopped the recording and went down and rounded up her parents. Since her unknowing confession, they had become very close. She shared a lot more of her life with them. She was excited as she found them seated with their day's activities placed on the shelf.

"Come, quick, you are not going to believe this. I recorded a program. You have to see what I found." The parents were not as enthusiastic as their daughter, but they rose from their seats and followed her up to the girl's room. She started the program from the beginning. There looking back at them was a spitting image of their long, lost daughter. Mom got close to Dad and wrapped her arm around him. He returned the jester. As her story unfolded and her desperate attempt to reach her dream faded away both exclaimed at the same time.

"We have got to go and find her. Let's do it tomorrow." Symphony agreed.

"She was calling out to me, just like Melody did before something bad happened. We have to go. Time is of essence. What time will we leave in the morning?"

"Let's make a day of it. We will

pack a lunch and take a road trip. We will find Rapsody in that city if it takes all day." Fortunately, she had given her last name. It was not Hill though, but Smith. To make it a bit harder, she would be living with her aunt who probably did not share the same name.

The following morning, they headed out. It was a beautiful, Indian summer day. The sky was cloudless, although that is not so unusual for Nevada. A slight breeze was blowing. In town, several of the homes that had landscaping around them had trees that displayed their full fall colors. Symphony placed the CD of their songs on to play. She would start the trip and later Mom, or Dad would take over driving if she tired. In short order, they arrived. They decided to start at the high school. Surely Rapsody had been a student there for at least a few weeks after arriving at her aunt's place. As it happened, fortune was on their side. Within a few minutes they were driving into the yard. Rapsody was seated in a rocking bench on the porch. She sprang up from her seat and went to see who her guests were. Her aunt was not married at the time and was working, the girl was home alone. As she approached the SUV her eyes became large as saucers as she looked at the driver. She was first going to go to the window where Dad was but hurried around to the driver's side right to the window where Symphony was seated. As their eyes met, the bond was instantly formed.

Perhaps on rare occasions in your life you have met someone who has had this effect on you. One look and you know that destiny is at work, that from this first meeting forward, your life will change forever. Symphony opened her door and in a moment the girls were in each other's arms. It was a miracle. Mom and Dad exited from the other side and stood arm and arm again-they had been doing this a lot lately-as the girls went over and sit down in the swinging bench. They were a carbon copy of each other. Had any casual observer seen the two of them together, they would have sworn they were identical twins. They were the same age, the same height, the same weight, the same build. For

Mom and Dad, it was something they would remember and cherish for the rest of their lives. For this union was as if their Melody had come back from the grave to be with them once again. The introductions were made, and they all took seats as Rapsody told of her experience.

"My little sister and I were close, as close as you and your sister Melody were, Symphony. When she came into my life, I knew it was my responsible to protect her at all costs. We were only eighteen months apart and looked so much alike, many thought we were twins although they could not understand how one identical twin was taller than the other. After she got older and closer to adult size, if she wore heals, we came pretty close to being the same size. When I got word of her death along with the death of my parents, I just about lost it. I had failed my little sister. I begged God to forgive me. They did not want her to go with them. But on that day, I had a big English project due and did not want to be bothered. I hugged her goodbye as always and told her to be safe. That was the last I saw her alive. You, at least got to see your sister before she passed. I would have given anything to be there as she slipped away but fate must have had its reasons."

And so, the afternoon slipped away. The four shared the lunch the ladies had packed and Rapsody added a few things from inside. When the Aunt returned, she was not unkind. As she compared the story of her niece and the twins, emotion showed in her face. She almost cried. Though she was an aunt from Rapsody's dad's side of the family, she also had lost a little sister in a terrible accident. She was amazed as were all how uncanny the girls looked together. Mom and Dad called home and stated they were going to take some time off from work to sort things out. Since their story had gained a lot of publicity, their employers were understanding. That night the girls did a concert together. Though she did not have a base guitar, Rapsody was accomplished at the keyboard. She had a synthesizer and put together an entire band for background music. The girls sang like angels. And so, arrangements were made for Rapsody to return with the Hill's and live with them, with promise, of course that they would not loose touch with the aunt.

Mother Vineoleen-through eyes of ancient wisdom-watched as Rapsody finally came home. There were going to be some changes in her life. Her parents had never allowed her to dress in jeans. Girls always wore dresses, and they were long dresses. No girl should ever be allowed to show her knees to the public. Besides, tight pants showed off too much of a girl's figure which might solicit a lustful eye from some young man. There was no dating allowed either until their daughter was seventeen. They had passed from her life just before her seventeenth birthday. She had never been on a date. Fortunately, there were drawers full of clothes Melody had used. All the jeans fit perfectly. Rapsody was a great addition to the band also as her keyboard and vocal skills were put to good use. Although she would never be the next American Idol, she had found her place in the world and in the heart of her new parents and sister. It was only after she became a member of the family that together the girls-dare I say twins-were able to write the tribute to the missing sisters. For it was not just for Melody but for little sister Harmony also. Perhaps that is what Harmony's parting gift to her beloved sister was. A new sister, a new home, and new parents.

I will leave you with them seated at the evening table sharing a meal together. The home of the Hill's was full again. The future was before these two girls. Would their similar looks carry them into adulthood? It is hard to say but for now-just for this moment at least-Melody had come home with a new name, Rapsody.

EPILOGUE

Apples Of Our Eyes

Melody, Symphony,
Rhapsody and Harmony
Four golden apples,
the apples of our eyes.
Where have you gone to
Melody and Harmony
Two golden apples,
the apples of our eyes.

If you think your up in
heaven Oh apples of our eyes?
Or you think your down in hell,
apple of our eye?
If you are in heaven
then say a prayer for me.
Tell old Saint Peter to
send you back to me.
Apple of our eyes,
apple of my eye.

If you are in hell
Oh apples of our eyes?
Tell the old devil that
he is full of lies.
God wouldn't send you
to a place like hell.
You were too much loved.
For we all loved you well.
Apple of our eyes, apple of my eye.

Melody, Symphony,
Rhapsody and Harmony
Four golden apples,
the apples of our eyes.

The robber came and robbed us,
Apples of our eyes.
Your no longer there in
the pupils of our eyes.
When we looked into the mirror,
we saw you looking back.
Now there's empty sockets
that's a sad, sad fact.
Melody and Harmony,
apples of our eyes.
Apple of our eyes,
apple of my eye.

What happens to the grapes,
apples of our eyes?
What happens to the apples,
Oh apples of our eyes?
The brewer takes the juice
from the apple or the grape.
And adds a bit of hell,
bends them all out of shape.
Apple of our eyes, apple of my eye.

What does drinking do
Oh apple of my eye?
It kills you really dead
and takes away your eye.
My sister wasn't drunk when
she up and died.
She made me a promise
before leaving my side.
So where are you Melody,
apple of my eye.
If your not in heaven,
I know I'll have to cry.
Apple of my eye.

Where did you go to,
apple of my eye?
Dear sister Harmony when
you up and died.

I made you a promise,
apple of my eye.
Then I went and broke it,
it took away your lives.
I ask your forgiveness
if your hearing my cry.
And know that I'll love
you until the day I die.
Apple of my eye.

Your still in our minds,
Oh apples of our eyes.
We never will forget you,
apple in our eye.
We'll love you forever,
for your deep in our heart.
Is a private chamber from
which you won't depart.
Melody and Symphony,
apples of our eyes
Your right there inside us
in a place that never dies.
Apple of our eyes, apple of my eye.

Melody, Symphony,
Rhapsody and Harmony.
Four golden apples, the
apples of our eyes.

What is an apple, the
apple of our eye?
Its just a reflection, a reflection
in our eyes.
Now your a reflection in
the apple of our eye.

We all are a Melody,
Rhapsody and Harmony.
We all are a Symphony,
an apple in some eye.
Sometimes the music changes
and gets out of sink.
Sometimes an apple rots
and breaks that golden link.
So if there is a heaven,
where apples never die.
There's got to be a spot
carved out for you and I.
Where were somebodies apple,
the apple of their eye.

Apple in our eyes,
apple of my eye.
Apple in our eyes,
apple of my eye.
Apple of our eyes,
apple of my eye.

Were somebodies apple,
the apple of their eye.
Your somebodies apple,
the apple in their eyes.

- THE END -

9 781965 126004